EARTH: 5000000000000
0000000000000 MILES

For Gail Lieb, who made sure I got to the bus on time.
—J. L.

RAZORBILL

An imprint of Penguin Random House LLC, New York

First published in the United States of America by Razorbill, an imprint of Penguin Random House LLC, 2022

Text copyright © 2022 by Josh Lieb
Illustrations copyright © 2022 by Hannah Marks

Visit us online at penguinrandomhouse.com.

Library of Congress Cataloging-in-Publication Data is available.

ISBN 9781984835512

Printed in the United States of America

1 3 5 7 9 10 8 6 4 2

PC

Design by Kristin Boyle
Text set in Burbank Big Regular

THE MONSTER ON THE BUS

JOSH LIEB

ILLUSTRATED BY HANNAH MARKS

RAZORBILL

Angelique liked school a lot.
She liked her teacher, Mr. Parker.
She liked her best friend, Cassius.

But most of all, she liked riding the bus.

Anything could happen on the bus.

The wheels on the bus go round and round
all through the town.

The monster on the bus goes, "yum yum yum!" all through the town.

The villain on the bus says, "EARTH WILL PAY!" all through the town.

The T. rex on the bus goes, "GRR GRR GRR!" all through the town.

The astronaut on the bus says, "FIRE MAIN ENGINE!" all through the town.

The wizard on the bus says, "PRESTO CHANGO!" all through outer space.

"This is a pretty interesting bus ride," says Angelique. "But we're going to be late for school."
"What can we do?" asks Cassius.

"This is our bus," says Angelique.
"Let's show them who's boss."

The kids on the bus say, "CHANGE US BACK!"
all through outer space.

EAT AT BLARGON'S DINER
-TWO MILLION MILES

The kids on the bus say, **"FIX THAT ROOF!"** all through the town.

The kids on the bus say, **"GO TO JAIL!"**
all through the town.

The kids on the bus say, "COUGH HER UP!"
all through the town.

SCHOOL

The driver on the bus says,
"SEE YOU AFTER SCHOOL!"
all through the town.

It had been a pretty interesting ride to school.

She wondered what would happen
on the way home.

The wheels on the bus go round and round all through the town.